In the Small, Small Night

In the Small,

For the Havlik cousins, who always make a warm and wonderful
audience, and who were there for the first tellings——J. K.

For my father, who was in the hospital——R. J.

SMALL NIGHT

By Jane Kurtz

Pictures by Rachel Isadora

In the middle of the night, when the stars are walking, Abena opens her eyes to find a lump beside her in her strange new bed. She pats the lump, but it doesn't go away. She pokes the lump, but it doesn't move. She pinches the lump. It says, "Wa!"

"What are you doing in this bed?" Abena asks.

Kofi sticks his head out from the covers. "My bed is too cold."

"Your bed is not too cold. Mama gave you hundreds of blankets."

"What if there's a giant mampam lizard under the blankets?" Kofi asks. "What if it smacks me with its smashing, thrashing tail?"

"Don't worry," Abena says. "We left the mampams behind in Ghana."

"I can't sleep," Kofi says. "What if we forget Grandmother and our cousins now that we live in America?"

Abena pats his head. "Don't worry. I'll help us remember." She reaches for her new flashlight and turns it on. "Pretend this is the moon. Close your eyes."

Abena closes her own eyes. In her mind she can see the huge moon hanging over her old home. An insect whistles. Fireflies flicker on-off-on-off and fried fish and nutmeg spice the air. Now she hears the storyteller's voice ringing through the village. "Anansi is a cheat!"

The cousins dance out of their round houses and run toward the fire, calling, "Come and say what you know."

"Anansi is a cheat."

"So come and say what you know."

"Once upon a time," Abena says.

"Time," Kofi whispers.

"The world was a small place. All the people lived in one village. Anansi lived in that village, too."

Anansi was very tricky. He was sure he was the wisest person on the whole earth. But sometimes in the small, small night he stayed awake, like you, and worried. He worried about who else was lying awake and thinking up tricky things to do. He didn't want anyone to be wiser than he was.

Finally one morning Anansi got a large clay pot. Then he went around to the people and animals—anything that could think—collecting all the wisdom in the world and putting it in his pot.

He went to the elephant, with his flapping ears. He went to the lion, king of the forest. He went to the rabbit, who hears better than anyone. Everywhere he collected wisdom and put it in his pot. Finally he knew he had it all.

"Now," he said. "I'm going to hang this pot on the tallest tree." He called to his little boy, Ntekuma, to follow him.

Anansi started climbing. But the pot kept getting in his way. He was struggling to go up, struggling to go up, struggling to go up.

"Father," Ntekuma called.

"What?"

"Listen with your ears open."

Anansi was angry. "I'm trying to take care of all the wisdom in the world so no one else will have any," he called down. "Don't bother me."

He struggled to go up, but the pot kept getting in the way, getting in the way.

"Father," Ntekuma called.

"Don't bother me now," Anansi called. "I have to do this hard work."

"But Father," Ntekuma called a third time. "If you put the pot behind you, you can climb more easily."

Anansi swished the pot to his back. Now he could climb up the tree so-o-o fast.

Suddenly he gave a tremendous shout. "What! I thought I put all the wisdom in a pot. But my little son just said a wise thing."

Anansi was very, very angry. He hurled the pot out over the treetops. Down it tumbled until it crashed into the ground and broke. Wisdom flew out everywhere.

Abena hugs Kofi. "This story I told, if it's nice or if it's not nice, I carry the story to the next teller. Are you asleep yet?"

"No," Kofi says. "Do you think Anansi is awake right now, trying to think of tricky things to do to other people who are awake?"

"Don't worry," Abena says. "If he is, we're ready. I'm very tricky, myself."

"Tell me another story," Kofi says.

"Once upon a time," Abena says.

"Time," Kofi says.

The eagle, king of the birds, spent his days floating high above forests and villages, tasting the wind. The turtle walked along muddy paths far below the eagle. "Hand come," the turtle would whisper as she moved her right leg. "Hand go," the turtle would whisper as she moved her left leg. "Hand come, hand go."

The eagle and the turtle were friends. But the vulture would giggle and shriek to see them talking together. "What a friendship!" he would say. "It will never last."

One day the eagle's mother died. Eagle sent messages that his friends should come and mourn with him for a week or two. All the birds started to pack—from the little sparrow to the owl, who sees everything. The vulture looked up from his packing to see the turtle coming down the path muttering, "Hand come. Hand go. Hand come. Hand go."

 "How will you get to your best friend's mother's funeral?" the vulture asked. He began to shriek and giggle. The turtle never stopped walking.

All the birds went back to their packing. But the turtle crawled behind a rock and watched. The sparrow flitted back and forth picking up little things. The owl kept stopping to look at everything. The parrot strutted around remembering the golden parrots on the scepters of Ashanti chiefs. When the vulture was busy trying to strut like a parrot, the turtle walked over and climbed inside the vulture's bag.

Soon the birds flew to the tall wawa tree, with its large, wide branches, where the mourning would be held. When they got there, food was all spread out and there was mourning, eating, drinking, whatever, whatever, whatever. Eagle moved sadly among his guests. "So," he said. "Where's my best friend, the turtle?"

The vulture began to laugh. "Your best friend is too slow. She will not even make it to mourn at her own mother's funeral." He laughed so hard he flipped onto his back with his feet waving in the air.

Turtle pushed her way out of vulture's bag. Hand come, hand go. Hand come, hand go. And there she was!

Abena carries Kofi to his own bed. As she walks, she sings. "When you think you are laughing at somebody else, that somebody turns out to be yourself, yourself. That somebody turns out to be you."

She pulls up the covers around Kofi. For a moment the room is quiet, except for some cars honking far away.

Kofi looks around. "Are you sure a mampam didn't crawl into my suitcase? Or a rock python? Or a slender-snouted crocodile?"

"Don't worry," Abena says. "I'm sure."

Kofi sighs. "You're not afraid of anything."

"Yes I am," Abena says sadly. "I'm afraid people in my new school will laugh at me and say that I talk funny."

Kofi pats her head. "Don't worry. Listen with your ears open," he says. "If they laugh even one little giggle, remember hand come, hand go."

Abena laughs. "All right, little wise one."

"Abena," Kofi says, "do you think our family will stay here forever?"

"I don't know," Abena says. "I know wherever we go, we'll go together."

"Will you be my sister no matter where we live?" Kofi asks.

"I will be your sister," Abena says, "whether we live in Ghana or in America or in tricky Anansi's village or at the top of a wawa tree. Now go to sleep."

Abena stares out the window at the small, small night. These stars will keep walking all the way across the sky until her grandmother and cousins halfway across the world will look up and see them, too. She closes her eyes, hugs her new flashlight, and goes back to sleep.

Author's Note

A friend from Ghana, Kofi Obeng, amused and entertained my children with these stories of Anansi and the vulture and turtle, as well as others. He said that the stories should go into one of my books, so I asked him to tell me more about what his village was like back when he heard stories as a boy. One day, when Abena and her brother popped into my head, I saw it might indeed be possible to weave Kofi's childhood stories and memories into a book. —J. K.

Library of Congress Cataloging-in-Publication Data

Kurtz, Jane.
In the small, small night / by Jane Kurtz ; pictures by Rachel Isadora.
  p. cm.
"Greenwillow Books."
Summary: Kofi can't sleep in his new home in the United States,
so his older sister Abena soothes his fears about life in a different country
by telling him two folktales from their native Ghana about the nature of
wisdom and perseverance.

ISBN 0-06-623814-5 (trade).
ISBN 0-06-623813-7 (lib. bdg.)
[1. Brothers and sisters—Fiction.
2. Immigrants—Fiction. 3. Ghanaian
Americans—Fiction. 4. Storytelling—Fiction.
5. Wisdom—Fiction. 6. Perseverance (Ethics)—
Fiction.] I. Isadora, Rachel, ill. II. Title.
PZ7.K9626In 2005 [E]—dc22 2004002106

First Edition 10 9 8 7 6 5 4 3 2 1

 Greenwillow Books